Pedro Martinez

THROWING STRIKES

by
Mike Shalin

SPORTS PUBLISHING INC.
www.SportsPublishingInc.com

Book design: Michelle R. Dressen, Susan M. McKinney
Cover design: Scot Muncaster
Photos: *The Associated Press,* Los Angeles Dodgers

ISBN: 1-58261-047-9
Library of Congress Catalog Card Number: 99-64074

SPORTS PUBLISHING INC.
sportspublishinginc.com

Printed in the United States.

CONTENTS

Pedro warms up during spring training in Florida.
(AP/Wide World Photos)

1

Making a First impression

It was early in the 1998 baseball season and American League umpires had just gotten their first extended look at little right-hander Pedro Martinez. They come away impressed with the new ace of the Boston Red Sox staff.

"Based on tonight, he's the best I've ever seen," Larry McCoy, who called a 12-strikeout, no-walk Pedro win over the Cleveland Indians, told Knight-Ridder after that game.

These were strong words. McCoy had been an American League umpire since 1971. He had called

Pedro made a big impression on American League umpires when he came to Boston for the 1998 season. (AP/Wide World Photos)

balls and strikes for pitchers such as Nolan Ryan, Rotger Clemens, Randy Johnson, Catfish Hunter and Jim Palmer. This new American Leaguer must have really been impressive.

"I've seen Nolan Ryan at his finest and Roger Clemens at his finest, and Martinez's control is beter than either one," said McCoy. "Martinez throws about two or three miles an hour slower than they did, but he throws his breaking ball for strikes more often than they did.

"He's also got a great changeup that he can throw for strikes. I can't believe that someone who throws that hard can have that good of a change. It backs away from the plate like a screwball. It makes his fastball look even faster.

"The way he can throw his pitches besides his fastball for strikes is what makes him the real deal."

Fellow umpire John Shulock also came away shaking his head. He called Pedro "the right-handed

Ron Guidry," recalling memories of a great Yankee lefty who was also small—in stature.

"Guidry threw the same way—bust the hitter down and in, throw the slider away, and then throw the forkball, and the hitter is gone," Shulock said. "Martinez will throw the fastball out of the strike zone so that he can bring the sinker back and freeze you.

"I've only seen a few pitchers who can really dominate—Johnson, Clemens, Guidry, Catfish. He's even with them, or better."

In summing up his first impression of Pedro, the umpire said, "He's got command of four pitches, and he can throw them all for strikes anytime he wants. He set up hitters as well as anyone I've seen. Everything they say he's got, he's got."

That's the way most people in both leagues feel about Pedro Jamie Martinez, who was 26 when he was traded from the Montreal Expos of the National League to the Boston Red Sox after the 1997 season, a deal which had people scratching their heads. The trade also left Pedro wondering about his baseball future.

Pedro poses for photographers at Fenway Park, his new home field. (AP/Wide World Photos)

CHAPTER TWO

More First impressions

On November 18, 1997, the Expos traded the 1997 Cy Young Award winner to the Red Sox—a deal for minor-league prospects Carl Pavano and Tony Armas, both pitchers. On paper, this trade had nothing at all to do with helping the Expos on the field. Instead, it was a deal that had to be made because Pedro was entering his final year before free agency. The Expos couldn't afford to pay him, so they had to get whatever they could for the reigning No. 1 pitcher in the National League.

Pedro won the 1997 National League Cy Young Award while pitching for the Montreal Expos. (AP/Wide World Photos)

The fact Pedro was traded was hardly a surprise—everyone saw it coming. The fact he was moved to Boston, which had lost Clemens the year before, raised some eyebrows around baseball. Would the Red Sox, who weren't exactly tossing crazy money around, spend the cash it would take to re-sign Pedro? Would they keep him for one year and then either make a Montreal-type deal after the season or, perhaps even quicker, during the 1998 season if they were out of contention?

If you listened to Pedro at the time, you would have thought there was no way he would ever sign with the Red Sox. He was openly talking about Boston being a temporary stopover on the way to somewhere else—perhaps to Los Angeles, his original team, where he could be re-united with one of his two professional baseball-playing (both pitchers) brothers, Ramon. Pedro had never wanted to leave the Dodgers in the first place.

Pedro likes the way people in Boston care about baseball.
(AP/Wide World Photos)

Pedro flew to Boston to meet the New England press. Something happened to him after he got off the plane which may have re-shaped his future. Pedro noticed the people in Boston—noticed how people in the airport, and the cab driver who took him to Fenway Park, lived and breathed the Boston Red Sox. Remember, Pedro had come from Montreal, where the fans really didn't care about his sport. This new attitude impressed him.

"It will be nice to pitch in a place where people care," Pedro said later. "I love the way people are there about baseball. That's the way it should be in every city. I'll take the challenge to go out there and do the best I can for the fans and myself."

As impressive as the fans were to Pedro, the incredible offer made by the Red Sox was even more impressive. Before actually becoming a free-agent, Pedro Martinez became baseball's highest-paid player (at least at the time) by agreeing to a six-

Pedro wants to be the first pitcher to win the Cy Young Award in both the National and American Leagues. (AP/Wide World Photos)

year, $75 million contract with the Sox—a deal that could grow by two years and $17 million at the back end.

The Red Sox had pulled it off.

In the span of less than two years, the Sox had bid farewell to Clemens, a sure Hall of Famer who would win his fourth and fifth Cy Young Awards with the Toronto Blue Jays in 1997 and 1998, and said hello to this Dominican righty who may just have Cooperstown on his future address list too.

"We're confident he won't be affected," Red Sox general manager Dan Duquette said of the contract signed by Pedro. "I mean, I'm very familiar with his family, his work ethic, his age (26 at the time). First and foremost, he's a baseball player. He grew up with it, lives it, works hard at it. He likes the attention, likes being around people and is highly motivated. One of his goals is to be the first pitcher to win the Cy Young Award in both leagues (in back-to-back years).

"We took all of that into consideration before making the trade," Duquette continued. "We knew the kind of person he was, as well as the kind of pitcher he was. We knew what it would take to sign him and weren't intimidated. We felt he was the building block we needed.

"This was a statement by our club that we're back in business. We wanted to show our fans that we felt we have a contending club and that we are willing to pay the price for the staff ace we needed. If you look at Pedro's career path, it's very similar to that of Greg Maddux a year before he went to the Braves (from the Cubs).

"He gives us an ace to our staff. He can make the rest of the team a lot better."

In his first year in the American League, Pedro, pledging that his pride was worth more than all the money in the world, backed up the words of his general manager. He pitched the Red Sox into the American League playoffs and made a real run at becoming the first pitcher ever to win back-to-back Cy Youngs in both leagues—only the second ever to win it in both leagues at all. He showed the Red Sox and their fans he had done his best.

Pedro grew up in the Dominican Republic with five brothers and sisters. (AP/Wide World Photos)

What This Guy is Really All About

"I believe I have earned the money, but that is not my motivation," Pedro told the *Los Angeles Times* after arriving at spring training in 1998. "The way I look at it is every time I pitch I have to bring food to the table. I have to bring food to my people no matter how I feel or if I'm hurt that day. I could be making nothing and I'd still have the same motivation."

That is what this guy is really about. The reason is his background, which is a far cry from a kid

In 1998, Pedro donated money to help send supplies to hurricane victims in Haiti. (AP/Wide World Photos)

from a rich family who plays in all the finest little leagues and gets all the best training only money can buy. This is a story about a kid and his brothers from an impoverished area of the Dominican Republic, who started playing the game by ripping the heads off their sisters' dolls and hitting them—or bottle caps—with broomsticks in a town with dirt roads rather than super highways.

It was a hunble beginning for someone who would later feel the pressure of pitching for his team—and his country.

"I think the pressure of being the No. 1 man from the Dominican right now is bigger than what I'm going to have pitching for Boston," Pedro said. "People are expecting me to do really well. They're praying for me."

People pray in a church back home that he built. Kids at the church can go to an athletic complex that is also was a gift from Pedro. That's what

Pedro is all about—remembering those beginnings.

When, after agreeing to the new deal with the Red Sox, Pedro said, "I'm a little ashamed to say how much I signed for," that's another product of the way he grew up.

Pedro Martinez was one of six children of Paolino and Leopoldina Martinez and grew up in the town of Manoguayabo, Dominican Republic. His parents divorced when Pedro was nine (they remained close and got together for family events) and, by that time, it was already clear baseball was in the blood of the Martinez kids— just as it is for so many people in his homeland.

Baseballs were needed, and, unfortunately, off went the dolls' heads. "My mom would be all over us, my sisters would be crying," Pedro told the *Boston Herald* after joining the Red Sox. "But that's what we did.

"When my sisters came home from school, they'd find (the dolls) with no head and they would go, 'Mommy! Mommy!' I would take anything that was round to play baseball. That's the passion I had."

***Pedro feels his belief in God is an important part
of his success. (AP/Wide World Photos)***

On the Way to Stardom

As the younger brother of a talented pitcher like Ramon, Pedro followed his older brother everywhere—all the way to the Dodgers. "I say Ramon is two times better than me," Pedro said. "What I know of baseball, and life off the field, I owe to Ramon.

"Everything I am I learned from Ramon."

Well, he may owe a bit of his success as a person and an athlete to someone else—Pedro is a firm believer God has a lot to do with all of this success.

Prayer is a major part of his life, which is the main reason he built the church in his hometown.

"I would like people to realize that God will give you things if you pray," Pedro says. "I don't think that my body size (he's only 5-foot-11) and my weight (about 165 pounds at the end of a work day) are the greatest for playing baseball, but I found that if you pray to God, he will help you. The best way I found to express that is to build a church and have people go there and listen to God's word."

Even though his nickname as a kid was "Angel," Pedro does not consider himself a saint. "I just believe in God," he said.

He also believes very strongly in his family. "When we get together as a family now, I'm the joker," he says. "I'm the one grabbing Ramon's ears, putting my mom on my back and running around pinching everybody."

Pro scouts saw the talent in Pedro at a very young age, the Dodgers signing him to a contract when he was just 16 years old. That was in 1988. He made his professional debut two years later. When Pedro signed, he was 5-foot-8 and weighed just 120 pounds. But he could throw a baseball. He was even practicing his English because deep down he knew he would soon need it.

Pedro signed a contract with the Los Angeles Dodgers when he was just 16. (Los Angeles Dodgers)

Off to a Good Start

Pedro's professional debut came in 1990, at Great Falls, Montana, in the Pioneer League. Right away, it was clear the kid, only 18, could pitch. He made 14 starts that year, going 8-3 with a 3.62 earned run average—and striking out 82 in 77 innings. The following year, he started to move up the Dodger ladder, reaching the majors in 1992.

In 1991, Pedro was a sparkling 8-0 in 10 starts at Bakersfield, Calif., in the Class A California League, compling a 2.05 ERA and striking out 83 while walking 19 in 61 $^1/_3$ innings. The call came to move to San Antonio, Texas 4:19 PM (Double-A) and he was 7-5 with a 1.76 ERA there. Pedro wasn't finished—he went 3-3 with a 3.66 ERA at Albuquerque, N.M., the Triple A farm club. Remember, he turned 20 after the season ended—and he was named Minor League Player of the Year by The Sporting News and Dodger Minor League Pitcher of the Year, neither a surprise after a three-team record of 18-8, the 18 wins the second-highest of any pitcher in the minor leagues and his 192 strikeouts fourth-best in minor-league ball.

Pedro began the 1992 season at Albuquerque and went 7-6 with a 3.81 ERA in 20 starts. He spent time on the disabled list with a shoulder problem that required post-season surgery—but it was on his left shoulder.

Before that 1992 season, Pedro said: "I feel like I was ready (for the major leagues) two years ago, but it's not up to me. Sure, I imagine making it now. You never know. I would take anything—starting, closing, long relief, I don't care. But they know what they're doing with me."

His numbers were not spectacular, but good enough and he finished the season in Los Angeles, making two relief appearances. He lost a game, but struck out eight in his eight innings. He was sent back to Albuquerque to start the 1993 season, but that stay turned out to be brief—one outing, a three-inning tuneup start. Pedro was on his way to the big leagues for good. He was 21 years old.

Pedro's first 1993 appearance with the Dodgers was in relief of his older brother Ramon. (Los Angeles Dodgers)

The Big Time

On April 11, 1993, in Atlanta, Ramon Martinez started a game for the Dodgers. When he was taken out of the game, the pitcher Tommy Lasorda brought in to relieve him was Ramon's skinny little brother.

Pedro went on to make 65 appearances for the Dodgers that year (two starts), going 10-5 with a 2.61 ERA and a pair of saves. His 113 strikeouts in relief tied future Montreal teammate John Wetteland for most relief strikeouts that year and were also the most by a Dodger since Mike Marshall

Opponents batted just .201 against Pedro in 1993.
(Los Angeles Dodgers)

had 143 in 1974. Marshall pitched 208⅓ innings—Pedro worked only 107. He gave up only 76 hits in those 107 innings, opponents batting just .201 against him.

The mark had been made and it was clear the Dodgers had themselves another Martinez that could pitch. Only it turned out that his Dodger career was over before it really had time to begin.

The numbers were good, the future was bright, but the Dodgers were deep in pitching and needed a second baseman. General manager Fred Claire traded Pedro to the Expos—and GM Dan Duquette—for second baseman Delino DeShields. The Dodgers are still regretting the move, but not as much as Pedro, who didn't want to leave his two brothers—Ramon. Jesus was also pitching in the organization.

"It's the kind of trade you stay up nights thinking about," Duquette told *Sports Illustrated* at the

Ramon, Pedro's older brother, still pitches for the Dodgers. (AP/Wide World Photos)

time. Added Claire: "It wasn't a trade for the mild-mannered. Dan and I talked about how we were going to get killed (in the public eye) on this deal. It was safer not to make the trade. But it made all the sense in the world."

Not to Pedro—or, for that matter, DeShields.

"They said I was the future of the Dodgers," Pedro said. "I was the one guy coming out of the minors who could be a starter. I could have been anything they wanted me to be. Look at the pitchers in their rotation (three starting pitchers 32 years old or older). How much future do they have?"

The deal literally came out of the Dodger Blue.

"What was so interesting about this deal is that no one knew about it beforehand except (Duquette) and myself," said Claire. "How many trades are rumored about before they're made? As a GM, this is the way you want it: Boom! It's done."

So was Pedro's stay in the same organization as his brothers.

Still just 23 years old, Pedro Martinez had to move on.

Ironically, when Pedro was only 20, Claire had watched him throw during spring training and exclaimed: "I'm not going to trade Pedro Martinez. I don't care what they offer. He has everything you look for, an outstanding fastball, an outstanding curveball, an outstanding changeup and a big heart. Under game conditions, he has great poise on the mound."

He was gone just a few years later. And, he missed his brother as soon as the deal was announced. The following spring, he said, "If I tell you how much I lose by not having Ramon by my side, we'll spend the whole afternoon talking. I really miss him and I miss my close friends, like Pedro Astacio, Raul Mondesi and Henry Rodriguez. Those guys were born and raised with me in baseball, so there's a lot that I miss. But the Dodgers sent me on my own, and I'll try to handle it the best way I can."

He was clearly going someplace where the people wanted him and, more importantly, knew what they were getting. Expos manager Felipe Alou was well aware of this little righty's ability.

"His stuff is as good as anyone's," he said—perhaps not even knowing just how true those words were—even though they sold Pedro short.

His stuff was better than almost anyone.

Pedro spent his first full season in the majors (1994) with the Montreal Expos. (AP/Wide World Photos)

CHAPTER SEVEN

Success in Montreal

It did not take Pedro long to show the people in Montreal they'd made the right move.

The 1994 season, his first full one in the majors, saw Pedro go 11-5 with a 3.42 ERA as he became a starter full-time in the strike-shortened season. Montreal was 74-40 and on its way to the postseason when things were halted. It was a young team loaded with talent that would not be allowed to mature together because of the Expos' financial problems—troubles that led to all of these young

Pedro compiled a record of 55 wins and 33 losses in Montreal. (AP/Wide World Photos)

players moving to other teams.

Pedro had a shutout among his 23 starts and earned a save in his only relief appearance of the year. He fanned 142 in 144⅔ innings and yielded just 115 hits while limiting opponents to a .210 batting average.

Just before the strike ended the season in August, Pedro won his last five decisions for a team that had baseball's best record when play was stopped. The 11-5 record started a four-year stay in Montreal that saw Pedro post a combined record of 55-33.

Pedro came close to baseball history twice that year, carrying a perfect game into the eighth inning of one start and a no-hitter into the ninth inning of another. The perfect game bid, against Cincinnati, was ended when Pedro hit Reggie Sanders with a pitch. Sanders, so sure Pedro had thrown at him—even though it would break up the perfect game—

Pedro and Ramon faced each other in a game for the first time on August 29, 1996. (AP/Wide World Photos)

charged the mound and started a bench-clearing brawl. It was one of several chapters in Pedro's career that resulted from his throwing pitches too close to hitters to establish the inside part of the plate, the area pitchers consider to be theirs.

Pedro started doing that early in his career—and his reputation for it spread quickly.

There were 12 ejections and three fights in Pedro's 23 starts in 1994 and Pedro received three warnings from umpires. He hit a National League-high 11 batters during that season and it wasn't even a full season. "I'm young and I'm going to make mistakes," he said. "People sometimes don't realize that."

Many felt there was a purpose to every one of his pitches—that his control is too great not to know where the ball is going. "I don't throw at hitters and I don't care what people think or say," Pedro told the *Boston Herald* years later. "I pitch outside as much as I pitch inside, but if I miss outside then I'm going to give up a home run over the middle of the plate. If I miss inside, maybe that's a single, maybe I hit someone. I have to pitch inside, but I can paint the outside, too. You can't be up there thinking one thing."

His new teammates in Boston knew of his reputation. "If someone drills one of our players, they are going to get drilled back," said Mo Vaughn. "It's nice to have that going for you."

Pedro's throwing inside probably developed from arriving in pro ball as such a little guy. He had to get respect. He got it—and, as the numbers took over, his throwing inside decreased somewhat. In September, 1996, Pedro was suspended for eight games for charging the mound after Philadelphia's Mike Williams threw at him in retaliation.

"I was 21 and weighed 150 pounds when I came to the big leagues," Pedro said. "I knew I had to pitch inside but I didn't know how and didn't have the time to learn. I had to try to take advantage of every opportunity when the Dodgers put me in a game. All I thought about was blowing hitters away with my fastball."

Said Expos manager Alou: "I just think a lot of people in baseball were doing a poor job of trying to understand a young pitcher who could be a real positive for the game."

Added Darrin Fletcher, Pedro's catcher in Montreal: "It's not that he's a headhunter, it's just that his control is a little off. He gets under the ball and he conks guys when he tries to throw the ball in. It's not like he's attempting to do it. It just happens."

***In 1998, Pedro returned to Montreal to attend an Expos
game on one of his days off. (AP/Wide World Photos)***

CHAPTER EIGHT

Moving On

Pedro never had a losing record with the Expos. In 1995, he went 14-10 with a 3.51 ERA and also pitched nine innings of perfect ball—but in a scoreless game. His team took the lead in the top of the 10th and Pedro left after Bip Roberts opened the bottom of the inning with a double. Mel Rojas saved the game and Pedro, who joined Pittsburgh's Harvey Haddix as the only pitcher in baseball to history to take a perfect game into extra innings, became the only pitcher in baseball history to get a win after losing a perfect game in extra innings.

In 1996, Pedro was 13-10 with a 3.70 ERA—just a warmup for what he would do in 1997. Entering that year in the final season of his obligation to Montreal, Pedro said he would listen if the Expos wanted to keep him. Deep down, he knew it would be his last year north of the border. He went out with a bang.

In 1997, Pedro was 17-8 with a 1.90 ERA. He made 31 starts and finished 13 of them. He pitched 241⅓ innings and gave up just 158 hits while striking out 305—the 14th pitcher in modern baseball history to collect 300 strikeouts in one season. He became the first Latin pitcher to fan 300 and was the first pitcher to do it with an ERA under 2.00 since Steve Carlton in 1972 (he was the first right-hander to accomplish the feat since Walter Johnson in 1912).

Pedro was first in the major leagues in ERA, complete games and opponents' batting average against (.184). The list of accomplishments went on and on. Pedro finished the season with the Expos and was then off to Boston.

"I made no money in four years (in Montreal)," Pedro said, talking about his contracts in comparison with other guys in the game. "I was gambling with my career every pitch I threw (in 1997). I think it's fair to get the money I am now to secure my career. I mean, they're not going to give it to me because they think I'm handsome. I've proven myself. I've done things to earn it.

"People talk about the money, but I've never seen a million dollars throw the ball to the plate. It's me, the pitcher. Think about that."

On his way to Boston, Pedro had to pick up the Cy Young Award. In an incredible gesture of national pride, Pedro tried to give it to his hero—former Giants' pitcher Juan Marichal. Marichal was a great righty in his day but pitched in the same era with the likes of Sandy Koufax, Don Drysdale and Bob Gibson and never won the Cy Young—even though he had a career record of 243 wins and 142 losses. Marichal was 25-8 in 1963 and 26-9 in 1968. But, Koufax, of the rival Dodgers, was 25-5 in 1963 and Gibson of the Cardinals was 22-9 with a remarkable 1.12 ERA in 1968.

Marichal has a well-earned spot in the Hall of Fame, but Pedro thought something was missing since he had never won the Cy Young. When he tried to present it to Marichal, Marichal respectfully gave it back.

"Marichal is more than a friend," Pedro said. "He's somebody really special to me."

The people who watched Pedro in that first Cy Young year were truly overwhelmed. "To see him every time out was just amazing," said second baseman Mike Lansing. "He literally dominated people every game at some point. Obviously, he lost some games. We didn't have enough run support for him, but he made people look foolish with every pitch he had.

"As the year went on, he was throwing a cutter (a type of fastball) more. He was throwing a four-seam fastball. He was throwing a curve and kind of slider to different types of hitters. And he'd throw his changeup to anybody. He doesn't care who you are. Right-handed. Left-handed. And he just would make the best hitters in the game look foolish."

One of those hitters was Mark McGwire, who came over from the American League over that summer and faced Pedro. In four at-bats that game, McGwire walked twice, struck out looking and was hit by a pitch. The count was 3-2 on every trip to the plate.

"He has such great command of all his pitches," McGwire said. "You can be sitting (with a count of) 3-1, 3-2 and it feels like (it's) 0-2. When you're sitting on a full count, you can usually anticipate what a pitcher is going to throw. But Martinez has such command of his pitches—and he has four of them—you have no clue what he's going to do. That's not a good feeling."

What was a good feeling for McGwire was seeing Pedro go to the American League, a feeling undoubtedly shared by every National League hitter.

Red Sox pitching coach Joe Kerrigan, who was with Pedro in Montreal, was thrilled to have him back. "It was like watching a kid grow up, developing compsure and control," Kerrigan said. "He's absolutely electric on the mound now. I mean, Greg Maddux has outstanding movement and may manipulate the ball better than anyone I've ever seen, but Pedro can get you both ways—with power and finesse."

Asked about Pedro's great work habits, Kerrigan said, "Natural talent seprates him from other guys. A 95-96 mph fastball and devastating chanegup—that separates you from most guys."

*Pedro, catcher Scott Hatteberg (left) and third baseman
John Valentin (center) meet on the mound. (AP/Wide World
Photos)*

9

A Smash in Beantown

Except for two brief stretches (the first one the worst of his career, where Pedro yielded 23 runs, 37 hits and 12 homers in 24 innings), Pedro's first season in Boston was magnificent—and he made a real run at becoming the first pitcher ever to win the Cy Young in both leagues in back-to-back seasons. In fact, it took Roger Clemens not losing a game after May to keep Pedro from a shot at his goal. His performance showed the people in Boston the new heavy duty contract would not have any effect on the way he did his job.

AL ALL-STARS PITCHERS

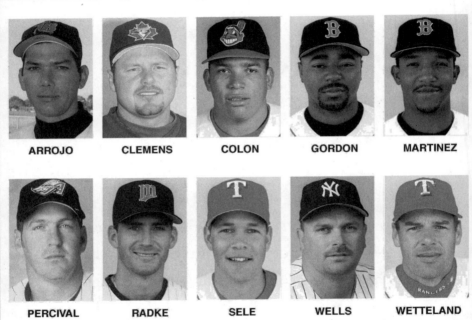

In 1998, Pedro was chosen as a member of the American League's All-Star pitching staff. (AP/Wide World Photos)

Pedro won a career-high 19 games in 1998, going 19-7 with a 2.89 ERA. He made 33 regular-season starts and won his first post-season appearance, beating Cleveland in the first game of the division series.

The Sox trailed the Indians, 2-1, in the best-of-five series going into game four, and Pedro said he was ready to pitch. But Red Sox manager Jimy Williams decided to take the chance of having the year end without having his ace on the mound. The Sox, ever aware of Pedro's small frame, didn't want to take any chances with their huge investment and ace. Pedro had had some shoulder problems—nothing major—and Williams and pitching coach Kerrigan felt it was best for Pete Schourek to start and Pedro to rest. Schourek pitched well, but the Red Sox lost and the season was over.

That decision was an unpopular one for Pedro, but he was even more upset after the season when star first baseman Mo Vaughn left the Red Sox as a free agent to sign with the Anaheim Angels.

"Holy cow," Pedro said. "I am really sad to see Mo go, because I really came over here to the team because I thought Mo was going to be there all the time. He was one of my biggest influences for why I am in a Red Sox uniform. To me, this is a big loss.

"I felt Mo was going to stay, I never thought he would go. I told (Duquette) ever since I got there to make sure some key players stay there, and Mo is the biggest one, apart from Nomar (Garciaparra). That's part of the reason I signed my deal, so I wasn't there bymyself like I was in Montreal."

"We're very close," Vaughn said during the season. "We're the guys who have to do the job, keys to this ballclub."

Losing a hitter like Mo can never be good news to a pitcher. But the Red Sox still had their ace, who entered the 1999 season with a combined record of 37-15 over the last two years.

CHAPTER TEN

It Was Another Great Year

Pedro's numbers in his first year in the American League were truly brilliant, even though he didn't match Clemens and win a second consecutive Cy Young award. But, except for that one little stretch, he was there for his teammates.

Pedro had some problems adjusting to the Boston fans he said he would love so much. It takes some getting used to when a group of fans is as crazy as those in Boston—and Pedro noticed when fans got on players. It was all part of an adjustment

Pedro seemed to tire late in the 1998 season, but recovered to help the Red Sox earn a wild card spot in the playoffs. (AP/Wide World Photos)

period—but 19-7 is a pretty good way to adjust.

Pedro was 9-3 at Fenway Park and 10-4 on the road for the Red Sox—then adding a 20th win in the playoff game in Cleveland. He made the All-Star team for the third year in a row, but, unhappy he was passed over for the start, he told American League manager Mike Hargrove of Cleveland that he would rather not pitch. That angered some people at the game—people who wanted to see the game's very best, even if it was just for an inning.

Late in the year, Pedro appeared to get a little tired. He lost three straight starts for the first time since 1995 but then stumbled to a win on September 24, the game that gave the Sox the wild card spot.

***Pedro shows his lighter side by wearing a Yoda mask
during a game against Oakland. (AP/Wide World Photos)***

People Really Can't Believe it

Pedro Martinez turned 27 years old just after the end of the 1998 baseball season. Officially, he was listed as being 5-foot-11 and weighing 170 pounds.

There were many around baseball who thought he was a bit shorter and maybe more than a bit lighter.

People wondered how that little frame could have that much power—and the one-liners about his size have followed Pedro since his first days in the major leagues. One-liners and compliments, of course.

Because of his small size, Pedro amazes people with how hard he throws. (AP/Wide World Photos)

"What really catches your eye is how small he is," said second baseman Mark Lemke, a Pedro rival in the National League but a teammate with the Red Sox. "You go up against Roger Clemens, even if you've never seen him before, and you say, 'This guy looks overpowering.' You wouldn't say that with Pedro until you get in there."

Houston star Jeff Bagwell once said: "The guy looks like Tony Gwynn's 14-year-old son out there and he's throwing 100 miles an hour."

Adds Larry Walker, a former teammate in Montreal and rival after going to Colorado: "You just don't expect a guy weighing 97 pounds to throw 98 miles an hour. He's just very aggressive. I never really watched Gibson pitch, but I get the feeling he's like a Gibson. If he has to throw one under your chin, he'll do it."

Walker, after spotting Pedro come out of the shower, said, "We're all talking. I said, 'Look at that

Pedro has a 37-15 record in two years with Boston. (AP/Wide World Photos)

guy. He weighs 87 pounds and throws 94 mph.' How does that happen? If they had air conditioning at Olympic Stadium (in Montreal), they'd have to turn it off, so it doesn't blow him away. "He's so tiny. And I don't know where he gets that speed from. That velocity is amazing."

Ask any hitter that Pedro has faced over the years, whether in the National League or American, and the answer almost always comes in the form of a compliment.

"You can't faze him," says Brian McRae, who came over from the American League to join the Cubs and Mets while Pedro was still in the NL. "We're hooting and hollering and screaming at him, and he just gets back on the mound and does his thing. Some pitchers, you can get on and it bothers them. Some guys get a worried look when the bench is getting on them. But he didn't care. He winked over there and was smiling. He jumped back on the mound and struck out the next three guys."

Echoed Cubs first baseman Mark Grace: "He's got electric stuff. He's right there with anybody— (Curt) Schilling or (Greg) Maddux. Maddux can make you look terrible but not by blowing you away. He does it with his changeups or hitting his spots. Pedro can throw it right down the middle and blow you away. But his changeup is much better than it used to be. Now he's got that same mid-90s fastball along with one of the best changeups in the game. That makes him tougher."

Here's a scary one: scout Ted Uhlaender said, "He hasn't reached his limit yet. With a team that will score him runs, he'll get a lot more recognition than he got before. The only recognition he got (in the National League) was from the players."

If Pedro continues to pitch the way he has the past few years, that won't be true much longer.

Pedro Martinez's Career Record

Year	Club	W-L	ERA	G	GS	CG	SHO	SV	IP	H	R	ER	BB	SO
1992	Los Angeles	0-1	2.25	2	1	0	0	0	8	6	2	2	1	8
1993	Los Angeles	10-5	2.61	65	2	0	0	2	107	76	34	31	57	119
1994	Montreal	11-5	3.42	24	23	1	1	1	144.2	115	58	55	45	142
1995	Montreal	14-10	3.51	30	30	2	2	0	194.2	158	79	76	66	174
1996	Montreal	13-10	3.70	33	33	4	1	0	216.2	189	100	89	70	222
1997	Montreal	17-8	1.90*	31	31	13*	4	0	241.1	158	65	51	67	305
1998	Boston	19-7	2.89	33	33	3	2	0	233.2	188	82	75	67	251

M.L. Totals 84-46   2.98 218 153 23 10   3 1146 890 420 379 373 1221

* Indicates League Leader

Active Career ERA Leader

John Franco	2.64
Greg Maddux	2.75
Roger Clemens	2.95
Jesse Orosco	2.96
Pedro Martinez	**2.98**
Jeff Montgomery	3.05
Jeff Brantley	3.15
David Cone	3.17
Randy Myers	3.19
Mike Jackson	3.21

Active Career Strikeouts/9 IP

Randy Johnson	10.60
Hideo Nomo	9.98
Pedro Martinez	**9.59**
Randy Myers	8.99
Roger Clemens	8.67
Eric Plunk	8.52
Paul Assenmacher	8.51
Curt Schilling	8.45
David Cone	8.42
Dan Plesac	8.22

***According to Chicago Cubs first baseman Mark Grace,
Pedro has one of the best changeups in baseball. (AP/
Wide World Photos)***

Active Career Winning Percentage

Mike Mussina	.667
Andy Pettitte	.657
Roger Clemens	.653
Pedro Martinez	**.646**
Randy Johnson	.644
David Cone	.644
Dwight Gooden	.642
Greg Maddux	.633
Tom Glavine	.622
Ramon Martinez	.615

Career Opponents BA Leader

Randy Johnson	.212
Pedro Martinez	**.214**
Mike Jackson	.216
Hideo Nomo	.218
Jesse Orosco	.219
David Cone	.224
Roger Clemens	.225
Jeff Brantley	.232
John Smoltz	.232
Randy Myers	.233

Hits/9 IP Active Career Leaders

Randy Johnson	6.93
Pedro Martinez	**6.99**
Mike Jackson	7.03
Jesse Orosco	7.16
Hideo Nomo	7.19
Davd Cone	7.44
Roger Clemens	7.51
Jeff Brantley	7.66
Randy Myers	7.71
Al Leiter	7.71

1990s National League Cy Young Award Winners

1998	Tom Glavine
1997	**Pedro Martinez**
1996	John Smoltz
1995	Greg Maddux
1994	Greg Maddux
1993	Greg Maddux
1992	Greg Maddux
1991	Tom Glavine
1990	Doug Drabek

Pedro Martinez
1997 Cy Young Winning Season

Totals

ERA	G	W	L	GSt	CG	ShO	IP	H	R	ER	HR	TBB	SO
1.90	31	17	8	31	13	4	241.1	158	65	51	16	67	305

Date	Opp	W/L	IP	H	R	ER	HR	TBB	SO
4/15	@Hou	W	6.0	3	1	1	1	2	5
4/20	@Phi	W	7.1	5	0	0	0	2	8
4/26	NYN	W	7.0	4	1	0	0	3	10
5/1	Hou	W*	9.0**	3	0	0	0	2	9
5/6	@SF	W	7.0	2	1	1	0	1	10
5/13	SD	W	9.0**	11	3	2	0	0	7
5/18	LA	W	7.0	6	4	3	2	1	7
5/23	Pit	W	9.0**	5	1	1	0	0	12

Date	Opp	W/L	IP	H	R	ER	HR	TBB	SO
5/28	NYN	L	5.0	7	7	2	1	3	5
6/3	@NYN	L	8.0**	7	2	2	1	2	12
6/8	ChN	—	6.2	6	4	4	0	3	13
6/14	Det	W*	9.0**	3	0	0	0	2	14
6/20	Fla	L	9.0**	5	2	2	1	4	12
6/25	Cin	—	9.0	5	1	1	0	3	11
6/30	@Tor	W	9.0**	3	1	1	1	1	10
7/5	Atl	L	7.0	6	4	4	1	6	9
7/13	@Cin	W*	9.0**	1	0	0	0	1	9
7/18	Hou	L	7.0	7	2	2	0	3	9
7/24	@Hou	—	6.0	5	5	5	2	1	4
7/29	@Col	W*	9.0**	5	0	0	0	1	13
8/3	SD	W	9.0**	3	3	1	1	3	10
8/9	SF	W	9.0**	4	1	1	0	2	8

Date	Opp	W/L	IP	H	R	ER	HR	TBB	SO
8/14	@LA	L	7.0	5	1	1	1	4	12
8/20	StL	—	6.2	3	2	0	0	6	13
8/25	@StL	W	8.2	4	1	1	0	2	13
8/30	@NYA	W	9.0**	5	2	2	0	1	10
9/4	Phi	L	8.0	7	5	5	3	1	11
9/10	Pit	W	7.0	7	3	2	0	0	8
9/15	@Pit	—	7.0	11	4	4	0	2	10
9/20	@Atl	L	8.0**	6	3	2	1	1	12
9/25	Fla	—	7.04	4	1	1	0	4	9

* Shut out

** Complete game

Pedro Martinez's 1998 Pitching Log

Totals

ERA	G	W	L	GS	CG	ShO	IP	H	R	ER	HR	TBB	SO
2.89	33	19	7	33	3	2	233.2	188	82	75	26	67	251

Date	Opp	W/L	IP	H	R	ER	HR	TBB	SO
8/14	@LA	L	7.0	5	1	1	1	4	12
8/20	StL	—	6.2	3	2	0	0	6	13
4/1	@Oak	W	7.0	3	0	0	0	2	11
4/6	@Ana	—	7.0	7	1	1	0	3	9
4/11	Sea	W*	9.0**	2	0	0	0	2	12
4/17	Cle	—	9.0	4	2	2	1	0	12
4/22	@Det	—	5.1	6	4	4	1	3	7
4/28	Det	—	6.0	9	4	4	1	2	6
5/3	Tex	W	7.0	5	1	0	0	2	9
5/9	@KC	W	7.0	4	1	1	0	3	6

Date	Opp	W/L	IP	H	R	ER	HR	TBB	SO
5/14	@Min	—	8.0	6	1	1	0	1	11
5/20	ChA	W	7.0	4	1	1	0	2	5
5/25	Tor	L	7.2	12	7	7	3	1	8
5/31	@NYA	W	5.2	8	4	4	1	2
6/5	NYN	L	4.0	8	6	6	4	1	4
6/10	@Atl	W	6.2	9	6	6	4	2	8
6/16	@ChA	W	7.0	4	1	1	1	5	11
6/21	@TB	W	8.0	1	1	1	0	2	6
6/26	@Fla	W	8.0	5	1	1	0	1	6
7/2	Mon	W	6.0	2	0	0	0	0	5
7/10	@Bal	L	8.0**	5	3	3	2	1	5
7/15	Cle	W*	9.0**	4	0	0	0	2	9
7/21	@Cle	W	7.0	7	4	2	1	4	3
7/26	Tor	W	7.0	6	0	0	0	1	6
8/1	@Ana	W	7.0	6	3	3	1	3	5

Date	Opp	W/L	IP	H	R	ER	HR	TBB	SO
8/7	@Tex	L	6.2	6	4	3	1	2	13
8/13	Min	—	6.1	10	6	6	0	2	3
8/18	Tex	W	8.2	5	1	1	1	1	10
8/23	@Min	W	6.0	4	0	0	0	1	4
8/29	Ana	W	8.0	7	1	1	0	1	8
9/3	@Tor	—	7.0	7	3	3	0	3	11
9/8	NYA	L	7.1	5	3	3	0	6	8
9/14	@NYA	L	7.0	7	3	3	3	0	0
9/19	@ChAL		7.0	4	5	2	1	3	9
9/24	Bal	W	6.1	6	5	5	3	3	6

*Shut out

** Complete game

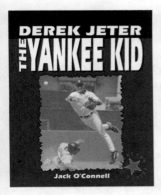

Derek Jeter:
The Yankee Kid

Author: Jack O'Connell
ISBN: 1-58261-043-6

In 1996 Derek burst onto the scene as one of the most promising young shortstops to hit the big leagues in a long time. His hitting prowess and ability to turn the double play have definitely fulfilled the early predictions of greatness.

A native of Kalamazoo, MI, Jeter has remained well grounded. He patiently signs autographs and takes time to talk to the young fans who will be eager to read more about him in this book.

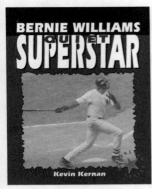

Bernie Williams:
Quiet Superstar

Author: Kevin Kernan
ISBN: 1-58261-044-4

Bernie Williams, a guitar-strumming native of Puerto Rico, is not only popular with his teammates, but is considered by top team officials to be the heir to DiMaggio and Mantle fame.

He draws frequent comparisons to Roberto Clemente, perhaps the greatest player ever from Puerto Rico. Like Clemente, Williams is humble, unassuming, and carries himself with quiet dignity. Also like Clemente, he plays with rare determination and a special elegance. He's married, and serves as a role model not only for his three children, but for his young fans here and in Puerto Rico.

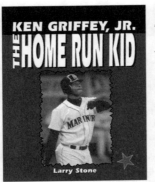

Ken Griffey, Jr.: The Home Run Kid

Author: Larry Stone
ISBN: 1-58261-041-x

Capable of hitting majestic home runs, making breathtaking catches, and speeding around the bases to beat the tag by a split second, Ken Griffey, Jr. is baseball's Michael Jordan. Amazingly, Ken reached the Major Leagues at age 19, made his first All-Star team at 20, and produced his first 100 RBI season at 21.

The son of Ken Griffey, Sr., Ken is part of the only father-son combination to play in the same outfield together in the same game, and, like Barry Bonds, he's a famous son who turned out to be a better player than his father.

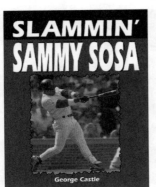

Sammy Sosa: Slammin' Sammy

Author: George Castle
ISBN: 1-58261-029-0

1998 was a break-out year for Sammy as he amassed 66 home runs, led the Chicago Cubs into the playoffs and finished the year with baseball's ultimate individual honor, MVP.

When the national spotlight was shone on Sammy during his home run chase with Mark McGwire, America got to see what a special person he is. His infectious good humor and kind heart have made him a role model across the country.

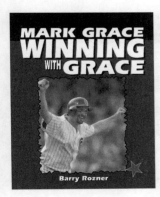

Mark Grace:
Winning with Grace
Author: Barry Rozner
ISBN: 1-58261-056-8

This southern California native and San Diego State alumnus has been playing baseball in the windy city for nearly fifteen years. Apparently the cold hasn't affected his game. Mark is an all-around player who can hit to all fields and play great defense.

Mark's outgoing personality has allowed him to evolve into one of Chicago's favorite sons. He is also community minded and some of his favorite charities include the Leukemia Society of America and Easter Seals.

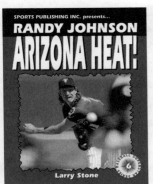

Randy Johnson:
Arizona Heat!
Author: Larry Stone
ISBN: 1-58261-042-8

One of the hardest throwing pitchers in the Major Leagues, and, at 6'10" the tallest, the towering figure of Randy Johnson on the mound is an imposing sight which strikes fear into the hearts of even the most determined opposing batters.

Perhaps the most amazing thing about Randy is his consistency in recording strikeouts. He is one of only four pitchers to lead the league in strikeouts for four consecutive seasons. With his recent signing with the Diamondbacks, his career has been rejuvenated and he shows no signs of slowing down.

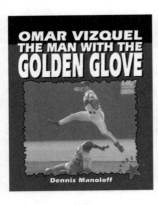

Omar Vizquel:
The Man with the Golden Glove

Author: Dennis Manoloff
ISBN: 1-58261-045-2

Omar has a career fielding percentage of .982 which is the highest career fielding percentage for any shortstop with at least 1,000 games played.

Omar is a long way from his hometown of Caracas, Venezuela, but his talents as a shortstop put him at an even greater distance from his peers while he is on the field.

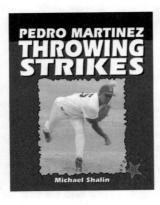

Pedro Martinez:
Throwing Strikes

Author: Mike Shalin
ISBN: 1-58261-047-9

The 1997 National League Cy Young Award winner is always teased because of his boyish looks. He's sometimes mistaken for the batboy, but his curve ball and slider leave little doubt that he's one of the premier pitchers in the American League.

It is fitting that Martinez is pitching in Boston, where the passion for baseball runs as high as it does in his native Dominican Republic.

♣

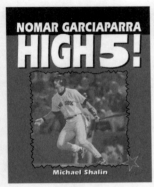

Nomar Garciaparra: High 5!

Author: Mike Shalin
ISBN: 1-58261-053-3

An All-American at Georgia Tech, a star on the 1992 U.S. Olympic Team, the twelfth overall pick in the 1994 draft, and the 1997 American League Rookie of the Year, Garciaparra has exemplified excellence on every level.

At shortstop, he'll glide deep into the hole, stab a sharply hit grounder, then throw out an opponent on the run. At the plate, he'll uncoil his body and deliver a clutch double or game-winning homer. Nomar is one of the game's most complete players.

Juan Gonzalez: Juan Gone!

Author: Evan Grant
ISBN: 1-58261-048-7

One of the most prodigious and feared sluggers in the major leagues, Gonzalez was a two-time home run king by the time he was 24 years old.

After having something of a personal crisis in 1996, the Puerto Rican redirected his priorities and now says baseball is the third most important thing in his life after God and family.

Mo Vaughn:
Angel on a Mission
Author: Mike Shalin
ISBN: 1-58261-046-0

Growing up in Connecticut, this Angels slugger learned the difference between right and wrong and the value of honesty and integrity from his parents early on, lessons that have stayed with him his whole life.

This former American League MVP was so active in Boston charities and youth programs that he quickly became one of the most popular players ever to don the Red Sox uniform.

Mo will be a welcome addition to the Angels line-up and the Anaheim community.

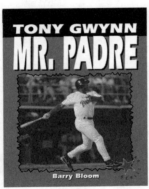

Tony Gwynn:
Mr. Padre
Author: Barry Bloom
ISBN: 1-58261-049-5

Tony is regarded as one of the greatest hitters of all-time. He is one of only three hitters in baseball history to win eight batting titles (the others: Ty Cobb and Honus Wagner).

In 1995 he won the Branch Rickey Award for Community Service by a major leaguer. He is unfailingly humble and always accessible, and he holds the game in deep respect. A throwback to an earlier era, Gwynn makes hitting look effortless, but no one works harder at his craft.

Kevin Brown:
That's Kevin with a "K"

Author: Jacqueline Salman
ISBN: 1-58261-050-9

Kevin was born in McIntyre, Georgia and played college baseball for Georgia Tech. Since then he has become one of baseball's most dominant pitchers and when on top of his game, he is virtually unhittable.

Kevin transformed the Florida Marlins and San Diego Padres into World Series contenders in consecutive seasons, and now he takes his winning attitude and talent to the Los Angeles Dodgers.

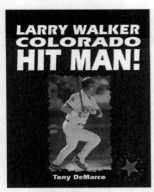

Larry Walker:
Colorado Hit Man!

Author: Tony DeMarco
ISBN: 1-58261-052-5

Growing up in Canada, Larry had his sights set on being a hockey player. He was a skater, not a slugger, but when a junior league hockey coach left him off the team in favor of his nephew, it was hockey's loss and baseball's gain.

Although the Rockies' star is known mostly for his hitting, he has won three Gold Glove awards, and has worked hard to turn himself into a complete, all-around ballplayer. Larry became the first Canadian to win the MVP award.

❦

Sandy and Roberto Alomar:
Baseball Brothers

Author: Barry Bloom
ISBN: 1-58261-054-1

Sandy and Roberto Alomar are not just famous baseball brothers they are also famous baseball sons. Sandy Alomar, Sr. played in the major leagues fourteen seasons and later went into management. His two baseball sons have made names for themselves and have appeared in multiple All-Star games.

With Roberto joining Sandy in Cleveland, the Indians look to be a front-running contender in the American League Central.

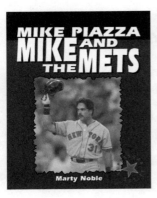

Mike Piazza:
Mike and the Mets

Author: Marty Noble
ISBN: 1-58261-051-7

A total of 1,389 players were selected ahead of Mike Piazza in the 1988 draft, who wasn't picked until the 62nd round, and then only because Tommy Lasorda urged the Dodgers to take him as a favor to his friend Vince Piazza, Mike's father.

Named in the same breath with great catchers of another era like Bench, Dickey and Berra, Mike has proved the validity of his father's constant reminder "If you work hard, dreams do come true."

Curt Schilling: Phillie Phire!

Author: Paul Hagen
ISBN: 1-58261-055-x

Born in Anchorage, Alaska, Schilling has found a warm reception from the Philadelphia Phillies faithful. He has amassed 300+ strikeouts in the past two seasons and even holds the National League record for most strikeouts by a right handed pitcher at 319.

This book tells of the difficulties Curt faced being traded several times as a young player, and how he has been able to deal with off-the-field problems.

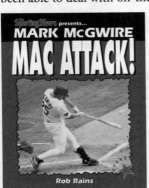

Mark McGwire: Mac Attack!

Author: Rob Rains
ISBN: 1-58261-004-5

Mac Attack! describes how McGwire overcame poor eyesight and various injuries to become one of the most revered hitters in baseball today. He quickly has become a legendary figure in St. Louis, the home to baseball legends such as Stan Musial, Lou Brock, Bob Gibson, Red Schoendienst and Ozzie Smith. McGwire thought about being a police officer growing up, but he hit a home run in his first Little League at-bat and the rest is history.

Roger Clemens: Rocket Man!

Author: Kevin Kernan
ISBN: 1-58261-128-9

Alex Rodriguez: A-plus Shortstop

ISBN: 1-58261-104-1

SUPERSTAR SERIES

Baseball
SuperStar Series Titles

Collect Them All!

____ **Sandy and Roberto Alomar: Baseball Brothers**

____ **Kevin Brown: Kevin with a "K"**

____ **Roger Clemens: Rocket Man!**

____ **Juan Gonzalez: Juan Gone!**

____ **Mark Grace: Winning With Grace**

____ **Ken Griffey, Jr.: The Home Run Kid**

____ **Tony Gwynn: Mr. Padre**

____ **Derek Jeter: The Yankee Kid**

____ **Randy Johnson: Arizona Heat!**

____ **Pedro Martinez: Throwing Strikes**

____ **Mike Piazza: Mike and the Mets**

____ **Alex Rodriguez: A-plus Shortstop**

____ **Curt Schilling: Philly Phire!**

____ **Sammy Sosa: Slammin' Sammy**

____ **Mo Vaughn: Angel on a Mission**

____ **Omar Vizquel: The Man with a Golden Glove**

____ **Larry Walker: Colorado Hit Man!**

____ **Bernie Williams: Quiet Superstar**

____ **Mark McGwire: Mac Attack!**

Available by calling 877-424-BOOK